Codes a

Written by Lee-Ann Wright
Illustrated by Peter Bray

Contents

Rigby.

HOUGHTON MIFFLIN HARCOURT

Codes and Ciphers

For thousands of years, people have sent secrets to each other. People used codes and ciphers to protect their secrets.

A coded message was often written on a belt. To read the message, people rolled the belt around a baton. The message said the enemy was coming.

OUYIOUN DANGER JB

3

What Is a Code?

A code is when you change every word or sentence in your secret message to a new word, sentence, number, or symbol.

If somebody wanted to read your secret message, they would need to know how you made your code.

Use this chart to work out the secret message on page 5.

A = 11
B = 12
C = 13

	1	2	3	4	5
1	A	B	C	D	E
2	F	G	H	I/J	K
3	L	M	N	O	P
4	Q	R	S	T	U
5	V	W	X	Y	Z

Try this secret code:

31 15 44 44 15 42 43   24 33 44 34   33 45 32 12 15 42 43
(Use the table on page 4 to help).

Here is another simple code.

Rules

Old Word	New Word
This	BLUE
Is	SHEEP
My	BALL
Secret	LUNCH
Code	ENGLISH
Can	DOG
You	JUMP
Read	SKY
It	ANT

Your secret message:

BLUE + SHEEP + BALL + LUNCH + ENGLISH.

DOG + JUMP + SKY + ANT?

What Is a Cipher?

A cipher is when you change each letter in your secret message to a new letter, number, or symbol. There are many different types of ciphers. Some are easy to break, and some are very difficult.

A simple cipher:

The alphabet

| A | B | C | D | E | F | G | H | I | J | K | L | M | N | O | P | Q | R | S | T | U | V | W | X | Y | Z |

Cipher text

| Z | E | B | R | A | S | C | D | F | G | H | I | J | K | L | M | N | O | P | Q | T | U | V | W | X | Y |

Your secret message:

BZK XLT OAZR JX PABOAQ BLRA?

Cipher Wheel

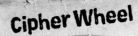

This cipher wheel was invented in 1467. It is made of two rings. The outside ring has an uppercase alphabet and some numbers. The inner ring has a lowercase mixed alphabet. The inner ring can move to change the code of the cipher.

Hieroglyphics

The people of Egypt used hieroglyphics as a type of writing system. Over 2,000 common objects represented ideas or words. It took a long time to write hieroglyphics and soon people stopped using them. After a while, nobody remembered how to write or read hieroglyphics.

Hieroglyphics were found in the Pharaohs' tombs.

Then in 1799, a special stone was found in Egypt. People studied the stone. They found it had three messages written on it. The messages were the same message but written in three types of writing.

This stone was named the Rosetta Stone. It helped people crack the code of hieroglyphics.

The Rosetta Stone was the key to solving hieroglyphics.

When people were at war, they used codes and ciphers to keep important information from their enemies.

Morse Code

A man named Samuel Morse invented Morse code.

Morse code is a 'tap' code. It is made up of short and long taps or dashes. Each tap stands for a letter of the alphabet, number, or punctuation mark. A dot means one short tap, and a dash means one long tap.

In World Wars I and II, people wanted to send secret messages using Morse code. The messages first had to be put into code before they were sent.

Morse Code

A	· —	I	· ·	R	· — ·	1	· — — — —
B	— · · ·	J	· — — —	S	· · ·	2	· · — — —
C	— · — ·	K	— · —	T	—	3	· · · — —
D	— · ·	L	· — · ·	U	· · —	4	· · · · —
E	·	M	— —	V	· · · —	5	· · · · ·
F	· · — ·	N	— ·	W	· — —	6	— · · · ·
G	— — ·	O	— — —	X	— · · —	7	— — · · ·
H	· · · ·	P	· — — ·	Y	— · — —	8	— — — · ·
CH	— — — —	Q	— — · —	Z	— — · ·	9	— — — — ·
						0	— — — — —

The Enigma

Before World War II, a German engineer invented a special machine called the Enigma to keep their messages secret.

The Enigma could put secret messages into code in more than 150 trillion different ways.
That's 150,000,000,000,000 different ways!

The Germans thought that no one could crack their Enigma code, but they were wrong. Code-breakers cracked the Enigma code. The code-breakers had a difficult job because the Germans changed their code every day.

Enigma machines were used by the Germans until code-breakers cracked the code.

Code-Breakers

Code-breakers had to be careful and very clever people. They had to be good at math. Sometimes it took code-breakers weeks or months to crack a code. Once a code was broken, the secret message could be read.

This man is sending a Morse-code message using light flashes.

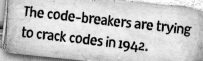

The code-breakers are trying to crack codes in 1942.

Glossary

hieroglyphics – an ancient writing system using pictures of common objects to represent ideas or words

telegraph – a system for sending messages along a wire over long distances

Index

Reports

Reports relate information, details, and events about a specific topic.

How to Write a Report

❯❯ Step One

- Choose a topic.
- Make a list of things you know about the topic.
- Write the things you need to find out.

Topic:
Codes and Ciphers

What I know:
Codes and ciphers are messages.
People use codes to protect their secrets.

Research:
I need to find out:

Who uses codes and ciphers.
What kinds of codes and ciphers there are.
Why codes and ciphers are important.

❯❯ Step Two

- Research the things you need to know.
- You can go to the library, use the internet, or ask an expert.
- Make notes about what you find.

﹥﹥ Step Three

- Group related information under headings.
- These headings may become sections or paragraphs.

Morse Code
- Samuel Morse invented Morse Code.
- Morse code is a tap code. It uses dots and dashes instead of letters.
- It was used during World Wars I and II.

Code-Breakers
- Code-breakers crack codes to learn the messages.
- Code-breakers are clever and good at math.

﹥﹥ Step Four

Use your notes to write your explanation.

- Introduce your topic.
- Add facts, details, and definitions from your research.
- Use quotations, examples, and vocabulary related to the topic.
- Support your report with visuals, such as labels, diagrams, and graphs.
- Use linking words and phrases, such as another for example also and because, to show relationships.
- Provide a conclusion.

▬▬ Guide Notes

Title: Codes and Ciphers
Stage: Fluency
Text Form: Informational Report
Approach: Guided Reading
Processes: Supporting Comprehension, Exploring Language, Processing Information
Writing Focus: Informational Reports

SUPPORTING COMPREHENSION

- Why do you think codes were used in war?
- What do you think an enemy would do with a message that looked like a string of letters?
- Why do you think the author created codes and ciphers for the reader to do?
- Why do you think hieroglyphics were put in the tombs of the Pharaohs?
- Do you think people had to be careful when sending a message in Morse code? Why or why not?
- Why do you think the Germans wanted to invent a special machine like the Enigma?
- What do you know about codes and ciphers that you didn't know before?

EXPLORING LANGUAGE

Vocabulary
Clarify: protect, baton, symbol, crack the code, telegraph
Nouns: enemy, message, symbol
Verbs: change, use, helped, invented